ANIMAL,

D

ISBN: 978-1-913642-49-5

Book designed by Aaron Kent

Edited by Aaron Kent

Broken Sleep Books (2021), Talgarreg, Wales

Contents

Animal, Vegetable

Roisin Dunnett

I am no longer baby I want power
_____

Part 1

'I'm Baby' was the best meme she had ever seen. Unqualified, forever: none would ever surpass it. Other things she saw on the internet, things that made her laugh or feel happy or recognised or guilty or despairing (for these were really the emperors, the fear, the lust and the rapture of the church of memes), none of them came close to matching what she felt when she beheld I'm Baby.

She experienced something that was akin to joy. The joy of recognition, such as a lover could provide. A sense of peace, like looking at an image of God: the truth, but also being told what to do.

How could she explain something like this to her parents? By the time they had grasped its meaning, all the concepts that formed the foundation of the image, it would have disappeared. They did not even know what a Kirby was. *She* barely knew it was a Kirby, in fact had mistaken it initially for a Jigglypuff. Now she knew it was a Kirby, however, it seemed impossible that it should be a Jigglypuff. That it should be a Jigglypuff would render it a lesser thing.

Her parents could not be expected to understand any of this, so she did not tell them.

To claim 'I'm Baby' was to to recognise your helplessness. Kirby, smiling with his pointer, recognised it in himself. But Kirby's announcement did not sadden him. In fact, with that little presentation on a pull-down screen, he appeared less to be announcing than teaching, instructing: *can everyone see in the back? I'm Baby.*

From a spiritual perspective, as far as she could tell, it was common and reasonable to proclaim yourself a Lowly Worm, blind and soft and slow moving. But to explain 'I'm Baby' was to crave some leniency. *How can I,* one could say, *when I'm Baby?* Like a child of god, but moreso. Sure, you could reprimand a child, teach it the rules. What could you do with a Baby?

She was on the way to a friend's house one night, late, drunk. Actually she thought that she might be a bit too late, so she walked quickly, with a bottle of wine under her arm. In front of her was a fashionable woman, a little younger than her. She admired how her hair was: all the way down past her waist. The fashionable woman had buffalo style trainers on, no socks. As she watched, the woman's Achilles tendons strained in the sick orange street light, in the blue and red lights of the chicken shop's illuminated chicken head. She was just trying so hard: so hard to get these gorgeous, major, shoes off the ground. It was admirable. But not necessary, all that strain. Not for one who was Baby.

The picture that went with, or was, or represented, 'I'm Baby' was set against a background of a blue floor and walls. You could only see a little of the blue, which framed the central image. They implied a corporate setting for the scenario unfolding. The scenario, the scene, was of Kirby standing beside a plain white screen. On the screen it said:

i'm baby

Kirby indicated the words with a plain white stick. Kirby had his eyes closed, smiling mouth open, like he was sermonising about the Good News. She had set the image as her wallpaper and her screensaver. She looked at it on the way home from her friend's house, much drunker by then. She switched to a video of a cat playing the flute. Then back to 'I'm Baby.' She was so drunk she nearly fell asleep, jerking up only when the phone finally slid out of her hands and onto the floor of the bus.

The next day she was very hungover, and one thing she noticed was that the sink in the bathroom of her flat was filthy. She got out the chlorine smelling surface cleaner. As she scrubbed the pale yellow crust on the sink she thought: *I shouldn't be doing this.* Was she not Baby?

Another time their kitchen was invaded with ants, attracted to the rotting, creamy effluence on neglected piles of crockery. The ants had it together: they formed neat and intersecting lines, carried each according to its strength. Her flatmates demanded something be done about the ants, and she did not disagree, but what could she do? After all, she was Baby.

There was a man she was seeing who she had been

intending to break up with. In fact, he called her *baby*. But he was mean and overbearing and she was dreading telling him she no longer wanted to see him. When she realised she was Baby, it occurred to her that she need not break up with him. How could she? Instead she became listless in his presence, and often fell asleep while they were together. She acquiesced to his desires, but showed no reciprocal interest. When he said something that made her want to cry, she let herself, not explaining what was upsetting her because it was too hard. She would just say that: 'I *can't!* Its too *hard!*' Eventually, though he was too possessive to break up with her, he left her alone, because she was fucking impossible to deal with.

She went to synagogue for the first time in forever to watch her second youngest cousin get Bar Mitzvah'd. Her aunt invited her to dress the Torah during the service, assuring her that it would be easy: it was not. She fumbled desperately with the ribbons and jingling caps of this most holy of texts for what felt like hours, and then shook a bunch of hands and retreated to her seat. When her youngest cousin's turn came, she tried to refuse, but somehow was tricked into participating again. She stayed awake most of the night before thinking about it, imagining fucking the task up in her stiff green dress, in front of everyone and specifically her grandmother. When, at the appointed time, she was invited to stand beside the pulpit, in the alcove where the Torah rested, she did so. But, though the kind elderly lady in a smart purple jacket motioned with her hands, her own hands remained useless by her sides, until the woman herself dressed the Torah. She went to sit beside her parents, who did not seem to have noticed. In fact, no one noticed that she had not done what she was asked. Her aunt thanked her very graciously afterwards as, after some prompting, did her cousin, who looked proud but profoundly fatigued, near collapse. It was shocking to see her, with that corpse like pallor, running between the adults to meet her friends, little frizzy heads, by the marble cake. Her cousin was a wonderful pianist, showing, apparently, great promise for someone of her age.

Kirby was a candyfloss pink videogame character, who came from the country of Dreamland, on planet Pop Star. Kirby was soft and flexible, could inflate or flatten, bounce high in the air. Kirby's principal method of battle was the absorption of an enemy's powers – Kirby would become engorged, like a puffa fish, by their acts of violence, only to vomit the violence, unchanged, back out at them again. Kirby was not a breaker, but a bender. Kirby had an optimistic personality.

Since adopting the doctrine of 'I'm Baby', she slept whenever she wanted to. If she was tired during the day she found somewhere to lie down and go to sleep. She let bills and rubbish pile up around her, and friends eventually came to her aid saying *Are you ok? I think you should think about talking to someone?* Some of the ones who had been through something similar, or what they thought was similar, said things like: *Look I'm going to come round and tidy your room, and then we're going to go through some of these bills together.* Some of the ones who were doing quite well said *What are your bank account details?* People cooked for her and took her along with them to parties and gatherings, and no one seemed to mind that she stood listlessly against walls, staring into space.

Some people in fact seemed really to like it, people were attracted by her listlessness. She exuded a void-like charisma and fucked extravagantly during that time, people who, in their turn, became drawn into the orbital clusters of people who did things for her, carried her around, met each other for coffee to speak of her in hushed and loving tones. She never paid for anything any more, not drinks or meals out or even most of her groceries. How long would people put up with this?

She did not lose her job in the cinema, but the cinema paid badly and required little of her. It was known to be a bottleneck for lost souls. No one commented if they happened to find her asleep on the floor of the staffroom under a coat: this was normal at the cinema, if the sofa was taken. When she was assigned to tearing tickets she would sometimes watch the films, many of which she had seen before, and close her eyes, registering only flashes of light and darkness as the projections illuminated her face.

She went to a talk by an artist she admired. The artist was witty, and full of an electric energy. Despite this energy, despite the artist's position (a position which involved mature activities, such as speaking confidently of her work to a room full of other adults who clapped politely and drank alcohol from glasses) despite all this she felt the artist understood something about the business of being Baby.

In response to one question the artist had replied with a long, deep sigh before saying: *Left to our own devices, we always strive for happiness. But that isn't always what we're supposed to do with our lives.*

She surfaced, briefly – was that what she had stopped doing? Striving for happiness? So what, then, was she supposed to be doing with her life? The artist had not indicated whether one should strive for something else, instead.

At the flat they got in trouble for letting a tree grow through their fence. The tree's victory over the landlord was satisfying to her, and she wasn't bothered when someone came and chopped it back – it would regrow. She didn't keep houseplants, and those that found their way into the flat invariably died of neglect, but she had begun to admire the universe of vegetation from afar: it seemed to be the only type of visible organism with true allegiance to itself, that could be neither bullied nor fooled. Increasingly she noticed the slyness of plants, gobbling up the poison in the sky, pushing roots into brick and chain link. Even being eaten was a part of their grand plan. Their patience was unbearable, their language incomprehensible. Their resistance was limitless. They seemed to hold no grudges.

She felt no kinship with the plants – their passive nature, if passive it was, bore no relation to the human state of being a baby. She couldn't feed off the sun, and was not patient but somnambulant. The new, slow pace of her life had, however, moved her closer to their frequency, and the lives of plants accordingly became more vivid. She took slow, drowsy walks, and looked at trees on the sides of the road, at weeds growing between paving stones. Window boxes, bursting with these mute, mysterious life forms. Her walks stretched out, taking her through parks, onto marshlands. She would squat down and examine the plant life, their sexual organs, obvious and mystifying, pulling their flowers apart in her fingers. They had no eyes, but they knew she was there. She knew they were more powerful than her and all her kind, and this knowledge reassured her. She liked weeds the best.

After work one evening she met friends at a club. She was bought a drink, then another, then another. Her cheeks went red like Kirby's cheerful ovals. In the crowd a kid had a small pair of wings, another wore a latex suit and had a melancholy, green painted face. On the stage, a creature with ankle length hair screamed into the mic while dancers gyrated in net dresses, their breasts and biceps painted with gold leaf. Everyone began throwing themselves around, the light flashing red and red and red and red and red she felt, once again, that she was tired and it was time to go to sleep. She thought that was what she was doing, just going to sleep, but actually she had vomited on the dancefloor: there was a pale, milky pool at her feet. A friend grabbed her and dragged her into the bathroom to wipe her face. Someone in a leather bra said *Oh my god...gross.* Someone else in tight black cigarette pants said: *Oh babe.*

The next morning she woke up in her friend's broad white bed.

Sun was trickling in through the blind – between its slats, she could see clouds moving. Next door, her friend Kay was moving sadly around in the kitchen. There was a cup of tea by the bed, in a sea-coloured mug. The duvet was so soft and so big, all around her like walls, and for a moment the softness of it was overwhelming, the beauty overwhelming, and she thought *home at last.* Then her headache made its first appearance. Nausea joined it on the stage, diarrhoea impatient in the wings.

Weakly, she picked up her phone and, through half shut eyes, began scrolling. She wanted bathrooms full of ferns, night time in the desert, nourishing images, but instead she fell into the algorithm and saw garish nail art, mac and cheese and Doritos, an unsettling, slightly sexist, cartoon strip. Then:

I'm no longer baby I want power.

It was a screenshot from twitter, just a line of text on a white background, and the icon was a photograph of a cat with tears in its eyes. She considered the text, slowly: *I'm no longer baby. I want power.*

She had never really thought about power before. Or rather, only vaguely and pejoratively, about politicians and known bitches, supposing that its pursuit was what made them do as they did. Why they became what they were. She thought being in charge of anything seemed like too much work for little gain, unless you saw power as an end unto itself. She had never, personally, tried to get any power. *Power.* Yet now it was a question she put to herself sure, maybe she did want it.

Certainly she had some power when compared with others who had less. But, she thought crossly, she did not *feel* powerful, and if she ever had, she had forgotten the sensation. She could not control what people did, for her or anyone else. She had been to protests against things that she thought were wrong (for before she was Baby she was something else, someone trying to Do What Was Right). She had yelled and waved banners and signed petitions. But such actions had made her feel more like a baby than anything: she would exclaim that something was unfair, and be ignored or punished, as if she were throwing a tantrum.

Kay came in with last night's make up and stoic kindness on her face.

-Are you OK? Do you want to throw up again?
-Do you ever think about power?
-Power?
-Yeah – like, if you have any, if you'd like more.

Her friend considered this. What else, on a cloudy Sunday morning, was there to consider?

-Sure I do… I used to think about it with my girlfriend a lot. Who had the power.
-Who did?
-She did.
-And if you had had it, what would you have done?
-Oh I don't know,

Kay lay back next to her.

-Shared it with her, probably. Like a dumb bitch.

It took forever to get home, bus after train after bus. She

threw up once at the end of the platform, and again into a plastic bag on a top deck. She knew it was just a hangover, but she felt as though her body was trying to purge itself of something more than alcohol.

When she got home she got out a notebook and wrote 'Power' on one of its blank pages, in bubble writing. She propped her phone against a glass of water and looked at Kirby with his pointer.

Her lunar calendar announced the Autumn Equinox. She looked out of the window. There was a bruise coloured door standing in the sky. Could she feel the earth moving?

Part 2

It was weird to remember a time before she had lifted her face to the rain and seen that door, bruise coloured, waiting in the heavens.

She kept the page, worn and faded now, with the word 'Power' written on it. It looked like someone else's handwriting. But then, as she reflected on rare occasions, it was a different time. Before the disorder and the mistakes that had come after.

She'd considered herself weak, which had been reasonable. How could she have proved she was anything other than weak, then? All the humiliations she had suffered were tame and she hadn't yet noticed her own curious prescience. She understood all that now but still, it was astonishing, looking back, that she had believed herself so helpless.

She hadn't known then, the story of her own survival. Of course now rumours had surfaced about the compromises she'd made. This kind of talk pissed her off. She'd never claimed to be a miracle worker, and at that time a life without compromise could only have been miraculous. But what about how, when shops were burning, she had found the courage to reach into the flames and pull people out? How, when announcements were made to a crowd, she would discover that the voice yelling above the hush was hers?

When the rain came for days and days, and the cold had gone right into her bones such that it couldn't be moved, she shocked herself by continuing to walk, one step in from of the other. She'd been Baby for so long by then. She'd not understood her own commitment to the business of living. She had believed herself to have given up. In fact she'd been in Power Saver Mode.

What if, when Jesus fed the five thousand, none of them had been really hungry? It's only when you've truly known hunger that you appreciate that story, and so many others: the gingerbread house, and the witch that lived inside. She had often thought of that witch and those children, each with their appetites. The step-mother, too.

Before the disorder began, she had already begun to think seriously about influence. Though her own suffering had not yet begun, the word was on that piece of paper, and she was ruminating on it. Her first thought was her looks. Of course, looks alone wouldn't necessarily get her anywhere, but they seemed a decent start, especially for a woman. The problem was that she wasn't sure if she *was* good looking. She had tried to analyse information about herself, the things that had happened to her. Were they the things that happened to an unusually attractive person? The results were inconclusive. She decided, then, that she was probably not good looking *enough*.

Now that she was older she wondered if even her averagely attractive appearance had been unhelpful. The uglier she got, the easier her role seemed to have become. People simply didn't trust a pretty woman. They didn't trust a pretty woman, and they didn't trust a young woman. Now she was neither, and people accepted her authority with much less argument.

The woman who came to see her, Josephine, was still young and good looking too. In former times she might not have qualified, or rather she would have taken steps to make her prettiness more obvious, but standards had lowered. She was dirty and her hair was roughly cropped and she looked a bit used up. It was because of the pollution, and perhaps the wearing nature of disappointment and pain, because their lifestyle was healthy enough. Josephine was steely and muscular, like they all were – no cigarettes, not a lot of alcohol. Plenty to eat, though never as much as too much, and it was hard to get enough protein, sometimes. There was a time on certain days when people could come and discuss their grievances. Over the years, people had came with all sorts of problems and questions. Josephine's was one that came up regularly, not often, but regularly:

-I want to keep it.

She stared neutrally at Josephine for a while, giving the request some space, before sighing extravagantly.

-You know very well you can't. Not if you want to stay here.

-This is my home. I want to have it here, at home.

She sighed again. The door of the barn rattled, it was autumn and the wind was strong, though not yet quite cold. The day before she had gone down to the reservoir to throw her sins away. Saving absolution for once a year seemed practical to her. Once a year was enough time to develop some perspective, decide what to hold onto, what to let go. Some wrong doings you had to live with for a while.

The yearly throwing of sin into water was encouraged in the community she led, but not compulsory. She wasn't that kind of a leader, she couldn't be bothered with people's religion. It wasn't the hill she planned to die on. However, the issue that Josephine had come to her with, that might be.

-It's the nature of your home that there are no children, no babies.

She was no pushover, Josephine, and she respected that. At her age, she'd not had Josephine's self possession or, honestly, her appreciation for life. Josephine was forthright and mentally seemed quite untroubled. It was difficult to picture Josephine in the landscape of her own youth. No way did she know, for instance, what a Kirby was, or probably even what a pokemon was. She imagined, briefly, explaining that when she was Josephine's age it had been possible to navigate the world through a screen which would reveal the imaginary locations of imaginary creatures, that you could then have pretended to catch. But this, of course, was not what they were talking about, and she struggled to return herself to the matter at hand. Josephine was speaking to her.

-I want to have this child. I have the right to chose.
-That you do.

Privately she disputed this. She wasn't against personal opinions, per say, but she'd always thought of the laws of her community as a 'my house, my rules' arrangement.

-That you do. You can chose to stay pregnant, and you can chose to leave.

-That would be a literal death sentence. There is nowhere for me to go. No nearby families will accept me.

-Well they might. Or you could maybe try and go it alone. Listen, I accept it's not an easy decision. I certainly accept that. But these are the rules. And besides-

She leaned back. Her shoulders were in painful knots, which she was attempting to loosen by rolling them around

-Why you would want to bring a child into this world I simply can't imagine. I thought you agreed with me about that.

-It's different when it's your own. You see things differently. You feel it here, She touched her midriff, *And here.* Josephine touched her heart. *-You must remember from when you had your own.*

-Oh my God, I don't remember that at all! I was desperate to get rid of her, haven't I told you? I feel like I've told you all about this. There was danger. Everything was falling apart. I was horrified that I was pregnant. I tried to get rid of her, I told you all this, but at the time it wasn't possible. I couldn't just stick a coat-hanger up myself!

-You could.

-Well, maybe I did.

-But even so, you love her.

-Of course I love her, what do you think? Of course I must love her, now she's here. But it has been a cruel life for her and it will only get crueller.

-She's glad she's alive.

-Because that's what she is: alive. That bit of indigestion, she pointed at Josephine's belly, bundled in a thick canvas jacket- *Is nothing. Don't let it become something, it would be a crime.*

Josephine looked fairly composed, but she was probably very angry. She had her fist around something in her pocket. What, a threat? But when she drew it out it was only an apple, and she ate it, in silence. It was tiring arguing with her, but she deserved that respect.

-Look, clearly you feel this is a difficult decision. Take some time making it. Two days, say. Come to me in that time, and I will administer the abortion myself. Otherwise, we will announce at the evening meeting that you will be leaving us.

-And will you say why?

-Of course! What do you think? This irritated her more than anything that had gone before.

-This isn't some secret underhand business, there is nothing to hide. I'm hardly shifting the goalposts. It's one of the founding tenets of our community. People here agree with me.

-I wouldn't be so sure said Josephine, sassily, and left the barn.

She leaned back and closed her eyes. She saw Kirby with his pointer. *I'm baby.* She missed her own Babyhood. Her phone was still in the chest pocket of her jacket. It was bound up with tape, and there was no reception any more, but if she charged it up on a generator she could look at her old pictures, and did from time to time. There were colours in the pictures that seemed, simply, no longer to exist. She had discovered that, left to their own devices, people would strive for happiness. But that wasn't always the purpose of living, and it was sometimes her role to explain that.

-Are you all right?

Kay's voice came from the darkness. She had been sitting behind them in the shadows, as she often did, and had not been noticed by Josephine. While people came with their disagreements, Kay would sit in silence and knit in darkness, using her fingers to count the rows.

-Yes, fine. I hate it when they come to me with this.

Kay had been with her since the first days. They found each other in a crowd along a motorway moving north. They'd not seen each other since the day in the bedroom with that terrible hangover. They hugged for a long time, and when she pressed herself away Kay said: *Can I feel what I think I can feel?* and she'd replied *Yeah* and Kay said *Wow, fuck.*

There were times while her daughter was growing up, so unexpectedly round, so unexpectedly pink, those bright healthy red cheeks, that she wondered if she'd borne a Kirby. Whether 'I'm Baby' had been a premonition, like so many others.

Kay would have loved to have had children herself,

but she had poured all that love into her and her daughter instead, claiming to feel lucky. Whenever she got drunk she reminisced about her old, lost girlfriends, and she still called herself a dumb bitch. The little Kirby hadn't grown up alone, there were others of her own and a similar age. Her bouncing cheerfulness had matured in adolescence into a resolute optimism that, to her mother, seemed almost psychotic. Josephine had been right, she really did love being alive. You had to suppose that she had some bleakness hidden in her. Still, it was the nature of people to keep secrets. Especially from their parents. Perhaps her daughter kept her grimness a secret. Secretively grim.

There was shuffling, scuffling now in the dark: Kay was putting her knitting into the pocket of her overalls and moving her hands around in the muck and dust by her feet looking for her water canister. *Want some?*

-No thanks

There was the sound of gulping.

-It's how a community grows, you know. New blood.

This was startling.

-It's not the time for that.
-Still no?
-It may never be. We've discussed this.
-But don't you think things have improved?
-I think we've got used to it. Made the best of it.

Kay laughed

-You enjoy life much more than you pretend to. Are you not proud of what we have built? Don't you want this to continue?
-People always come. That's how we replenish ourselves, by pilgrimage, not by birth.
-And if they stop coming?
-Then that's the answer. It's over. It'll be as it should be.
-You've gotten very conservative with age.
-That's what happens.

Later that day she watched through a window as Josephine swaggered around in the yard. She was eating a piece of bread slowly, letting its crumbs soften and settle into her tongue. She could feel the sighing of air in the dough as she pressed it against the roof of her mouth. She noted, spotting a long brown line, almost polite in its inconspicuousness, that ants had returned. While others in the group were at pains to keep them out, she'd maintained her admiration for them. Ants seemed not to have let recent events in human history concern them at all, although she supposed she had no way of consulting them about that. They continued as before. But then, largely, so did she. Outside, Josephine was digging resolutely into the earth, golden rays of the setting sun blinking on the spade's edge. You could tell from the set of her feet: she would have the abortion, and never forgive it.

To get her feet in her boots she had to wrap them with rags. The boots were too large, or her feet were too small, and they got cold too these days, a little blue. She was headed for the cracked basin of the reservoir, where sometimes they caught little muddy fish and grabbed indeterminate molluscs from the submerged, weedy rubble. There was no mist, it had all burned off since the morning, but the air smelled of smoke.

With her hand she parted the nettles and the brambles, the small fragile flowers on the end of grasses dripping water from the afternoon's rain. The summers got longer every year, and the summer wildflowers lived long, strange lives. Spots and speckles of yellow jumped out from the ground, mists of green and white shook water onto her shoulders. Violet and blues arranged themselves along stems like vertebrae. And so much pink! Late blackberries vomited from bushes into her path and she picked them as she walked, staining her fingers. They popped on her tongue like caviar.

There was a type of fleshy grass that grew on the dry banks of the reservoir in the baking summers. When cold weather came and the reservoir's level rose, the grasses endured, waving under their fresh covering of freezing water, avid greenness shining through the murk. Every year, this miracle. She squatted down, as she usually did, to gaze at them, her old friends. As she did so, there was a noise behind her. An animal approaching perhaps, though there were few around: nothing larger than a bird or a cat.

The dusk brewed, the sky's colour darkening. She remembered, out of nowhere, the neon lights illuminating the shape of a head of a chicken. The moon was thickening like butter, she turned her head up to look at it: a flash of heel and tendon in the night sky. Above her, as if it had never left, was the bruise coloured door.

'Oh what *now*?' she asked.

The Clot

The piping behind the toilet had brought damp into the wall: white, grey and pinkish flakes of plaster peeled away from the bricks to form an irregular pattern and the impression of disease. She heaved violently, almost hitting her chin on the toilet seat. She had been caught off guard, a little taken aback by the force of it. You never knew what to expect of the body she thought, adjusting her footing on the bathroom tiles. Always full of surprises. *Come on.* She replaced her fingers and moved them around, *this is boring.*

She braced herself for the next spasm, and something solid blocked her windpipe before sliding, whole, over her hand and into the quagmire below. Her immediate, horrible thought was that it was a bubble of blood that had come away inside her, or even an organ or a chunk of organ that she had unintentionally pulled out of herself. Was she going to die now? She wondered whether she was going to have to reach down and pull the thing out of the toilet, to present to medical professionals, but then the whatever-it-was surfaced, rolled over, and began to move.

Someone else, seeing this, might have been sick again, but that reflex in her was destroyed. Instead she immediately slammed the lid of the toilet down and flushed. She sat on the floor and breathed deeply. By the time the sound of water stopped she was convinced that she had imagined the moving thing: it had just been an unexpectedly large piece of food. She washed her hands and face and brushed her teeth. She sat down again, on the toilet this time, and took a few more deep breaths.

She had chores to do around the house. She attacked the vine that grew in psychotic abundance out of a corner of their garden, reaching through the kitchen door and into the bedroom windows above. It had wound sticky and astonishingly strong tendrils round the cupboard handles and she winced as she snipped them away, wide leaves falling to the linoleum floor. She swept the leaves up and threw them back into the garden where, presumably, they would rot and be gobbled back up by the vine.

She returned to the bathroom, and looked down into the toilet with practically no trepidation. Unfortunately, the thing was still there, a Clot, clinging now with irregular protuberances to the sides of the bowl, just in front of the hole leading to the sewage pipe. She surveyed it grimly, measuring the virtues of a succession of possible actions.

In the end she fished the Clot out, cringing, and dropped it into the bathroom sink. There were still pieces of food clinging to it, so she ran the tap over its body while it squished and stretched against the porcelain. It looked completely revolting, and she wondered how she could bear to look at it. Yet, somehow, she didn't feel completely unprepared for this turn of events. She wasn't thrilled, but she was OK.

The Clot rested by the plughole. It wasn't clear what about it indicated cognisance, but something did. It seemed keen not to be washed away but other than that, its intentions, if it had any, were obscure.

'Hello' she said to the Clot.

It had no visible eyes, no visible ears, no visible mouth, and she was not surprised that it did not respond. She sat down and rested her elbows on her knees. The floor of the bathroom was, viewed close up, nearly as bad as the Clot. There were balls of hair and dust, and tiny slivers of glass from a mirror they had smashed six months ago. The tiles also had a thin veneer of mud and crushed leaves: because the shower was blocked and always overflowing the floor was always a little bit damp, pulling muck off of everyone's shoes in the winter, from their bare feet in the summer. There was a tideline of scum around the shower, and some cleaning rags balled up behind the toilet. She forced herself to return to the issue of the thing in the sink. Already she was beginning to sense that, if she couldn't get rid of it, she must take responsibility for it. After all, she had drawn it up from the well of her body. It hadn't asked to come. There was a knock on the door and she jumped, a hard physical movement, and knocked her head on the cream coloured tiles behind her. She yelled.

'Sorry! Sorry.' said her housemate Hartley, whose voice was already moving away from the door. 'I wasn't sure if you were in there.'

She would have to think of some way to get it out of the bathroom without it being seen. She called out to Hartley, trying to keep any note of panic from her voice, but it emerged thin and tinny. She noticed that her hands were shaking as she scooped the Clot up in a wad of toilet paper and put it into the mirror-fronted bathroom cupboard, which refused to close properly.

'Do you want to have dinner together and watch a film?' called Hartley, clattering pans in the kitchen downstairs.

They made noodles for dinner, swimming brownly in sesame and soy. While they were cooking, she sneaked back upstairs and transferred the Clot to her bedroom. She knew she seemed distracted and weird at first, but as she calmed down their conversation became more natural. They left the back door open because it was a hot night. She was vaguely happy then: eating, gently sweating with the warm, gently sweating body of Hartley beside her. They shared a glass of something that fizzed, tasting faintly of juniper. Now and again she discreetly put her hand to her mouth, to see if there was blood.

She had placed the thing in a bowl, adding a centimetre of water. She resolved that if the water was gone in 24 hours she would put in more, and if it was still there she would tip it out. She had done a bit of research into what the thing might be, but was afraid to type too much, to delve too deeply into the questions and topics associated with her searches, because of not wanting to discover that she was dying. Haematemesis was a friendly greeting of a word, a smiling sound, and meant the vomiting of blood. Vomiting Animal was a gif, Vomiting Bug was Norovirus. She thought of her ex, who had become very involved in occult practice before their relationship ended in a splendid festival of acrimony. She had her suspicions. She made a plan to visit the esoteric book-shop they had used to frequent and ask some questions. Hartley would want to take her to the hospital, so she didn't tell Hartley.

Just as she was falling asleep she remembered when she had seen something like the Clot before. Years ago, at a music festival. She had guided her friend, who'd taken a bad pill, back to their tent through waist deep mud. It was Saturday night, and the barren fields of the festival looked like the site of some deranged battle: mounds of sentient sequins hauling themselves through the swamp-like fields, semi naked figures stranded on patches of burnt grass. Here and there teenagers in high visibility vests poured water into someone's face or ran by a tent shouting into a radio. There was hellish music everywhere. They had to stop several times for her friend to throw up, or for them both to reconcile their thoughts enough to continue moving. Back at their camp-site her friend made a final helpless meowing sound, vomiting directly by the entrance flap, before collapsing sideways into the tent. She alone saw the pale thing come out of her friend's mouth before creeping away into the mud. At the time she thought it was a hallucination. But perhaps everyone had a comprehending Clot deep in their bellies that, with great disturbance, could be dislodged? She fell asleep, feeling not completely dissatisfied with this memory, though mystified as to its implications.

The next day she had work to do at a reception desk in the City. She peeled herself, naked and sweating, off the filthy duvet in her bedroom and got in the horrible shower. She left wet footprints in the scum on the floor. She put on a very white shirt that she had ironed. She rolled up a suit jacket and put it in her rucksack. She held the button down on a deodorant aerosol for a good long time, until her armpits felt like they might freeze and drop off her body like treated verrucas. She located some ugly trousers and put them on.

She signed in on the ground floor of a colossal building, and was directed into a lift without buttons. It was smooth and white, like the inside of a shell. There was one mirrored panel directly in front of the doors, and it was while looking into this panel she discovered that, at some point in transit, her nose had bled, and there was a brown crust between her nostril and her upper lip. The mirror was here to facilitate discoveries like this one. The lift appeared not to be moving, and the doors made no sound when they cleaved apart on the sixty sixth floor.

There was no one else at or near the reception desk. There was a password written on a sticky note, taped to her monitor, which she used to sign in. Beside her, a news channel played on mute: buildings on fire. Eventually she made a cup of coffee and, ignoring the ghosts of outlook messages appearing and fading at the corner of the computer screen, she opened her personal email.

She typed

re: Curse

She typed

Listen you Fucker

Then deleted it. This wasn't like her. The words had emerged, like the Clot, unexpectedly. She tried again:

You absolute Cunt.

She deleted this too and held her breath for a few moments. The cursor kept time, neutrally, blinking with the regularity of a metronome.

Hi.

I know there's no point in contacting you about this, but I just wanted you to know that something weird happened to me last night and I'm 95% certain that you are responsible.

If you wanted a reaction you have succeeded: I am fucking furious, also grossed out. I'm sure that, in order to attack me in this way, you have once again called upon arcane forces that you cannot control and, as always, I will have to deal with the fallout of that.

I have had enough of your manipulative and irresponsible behaviour and am planning to both make you accountable for your actions and also have actual revenge.

Watch out.

She added five eye emojis to the bottom of the email and hovered the cursor over the button to send. Her heart was beating very quickly.

When she got home she had another long shower and got ready to go out. She wore a blue skirt, its waistband drew a line of sweat on her midriff. She painted blue around her eyes, and on her nails. She stood in front of her mirror for a while. It was too hot to bother with lashes, she decided. The Clot seemed to have taken up the water in the bowl, or it had evaporated in the heat? She added more. It still looked moist and sticky. She couldn't bring herself to touch it again, but the first time it had been the precise heat of her own body. She tipped the bowl slightly; it held itself in place. What was its desire? If it was a curse, what cruelty would it enact?

She knew the venue pretty well; she'd been there several times before. It had a concrete floor, and in the winter the audience had to huddle together in the seats for warmth, but at this time of year it was nice to see stars between the corrugated metal sheets of the roof. Someone bought her a drink, the beer came with a sharp segment of lime crushed into the bottle's neck. Her thoughts were half on the Clot, half on the performance that was coming. Suddenly she felt a sharp pain, like a wire, in the back of her brain, and another in her pelvis. She gripped the peeling varnished corner of the bar: *Jesus* she thought. Then it was her turn to get on stage.

Her performance was just before the interval, so the applause was extra loud because of the audience's sense of release. She was sweating more than ever from the stage lights and the pain, which had raced through twice more while she was performing. When she got off the stage her ex was there. They hugged and she felt the wet fabric under her armpits pressing against them both. Someone got her another beer, and she gripped the wet label of the bottle, and whenever she laughed she felt her lips dragging over her teeth. A while later she went for a cigarette. Her ex was out there too, wearing a big dumb coat despite the heat and sitting on the steps of one of the shuttered buildings near the venue. She was surprised to discover that her anger was immense.

She hissed at her ex, who replied with mild (perhaps false) surprise and veiled malice. She wasn't sure what to do next. She could feel tears of anger forcing themselves out of her eyes. Was there an incantation, some kind of power she could call on? What she really wanted to do was be sick at their feet, on their feet, as a gesture of disgust. She wanted to shout HAEMATEMESIS and vomit a bellyful of blood.

Her ex's eyes had a cold and familiar tint: like radishes in white vinegar. Their warning glinted in the dark, and suddenly she was really frightened, and turned, and walked away, under the hot dark purple sky, holding her skirt in both hands so it wouldn't drag on the ground. There was thunder, and rain the temperature of spit started to come down.

Back home she had a cigarette out of her window before bed, staring into the garden below, replaying the events of the evening and trying to do her breathing. Then she took off all her clothes and got onto (it was too hot to get into) bed. She woke up before dawn, and for a moment she thought the sound was Hartley going to the loo, or some other common disturbance. But then it came again: like the sound an oyster makes when burned with hot sauce. Like a church choir. Like the recordings NASA had made of electromagnetic waves round Venus. She felt incredibly frightened, and incredibly naked. The sound was coming from the Clot. She thought it must be singing.

The next morning she was very freaked out. But it was time to go to the reception desk again. She sat at the desk in the high tower, so tired it felt as though her brain was burning, slowly, like her skull was a brazier. Or perhaps that was the curse. One of the men who worked for the company came out and asked her to book him a meeting room. He dawdled by the desk, as people tended to. They wanted her to give them something, but they weren't usually sure what. He asked if she remembered his name. She told him she didn't. She was worried that Hartley, who had a half day that day, would wander into her room and find the Clot.

When she got back home, she squatted over the toilet and pulled the blood-filled silicone cup from where it had been resting, patiently, beneath her cervix. She pictured the instructive diagrams for the cup's removal, which had been clean-lined and elegant: the hands tulip-like, as was the cup. As usual, when she gamely clawed the thing out of herself, she felt a hot spout of gore over her palm. She carried what was left carefully into her room and dripped it in the bowl were the Clot was. There was a sense of recoiling. *Fair enough,* she thought. She fell asleep quickly and deeply that night, landing in a disturbing sepia landscape. She woke up to find her crotch damp and sticky with blood.

The Clot had pulled itself onto the bed, spreading over the duvet like a plant or an animal searching for nourishment. She yelled, and pulled her feet away from the end of the bed. It retracted back to its normal size and lay, soft and sticky on the duvet. *I should chuck you out of the window* she thought, but she couldn't bring herself too. Now it had brought itself back in, it seemed so small and vulnerable.

That day was Saturday and, as she had promised herself, she got on the bus to the esoteric book shop to ask some questions. She thought about taking the Clot out with her but the prospect, for whatever reason, was extremely stressful. After wrestling with the idea for a while she took some pictures of it, studying them with some disappointment. It looked like a recipe that had gone a bit wrong.

She had on very large, very tight black underwear. Black trainers, a long black skirt and a black hoodie. There were several shops that she and her ex had used to visit, which sold the kinds of books they had become so interested in, but her favourite smelled of pine, had workshops in the basement, and tasteful displays of stones and candles in the window. She pretended to consult a book about tea leaf reading for a while, scanning the shopfloor over the edge of the pages. Eventually she overcame her embarrassment for long enough to get over to the counter and speak with the shop assistant, who was slim and distant, had strangely shaped and quite intriguing teeth.

She spoke for a long time, explaining the nature of her relationship, their violent division and certain relevant details of the work they had been doing together. She took her time before getting to the Clot, making quick glances around her to make sure that no one was overhearing. Then she got out her phone and waited patiently as the assistant scrolled through her photos. The assistant was clearly sympathetic to her situation, but also somewhat at a loss as to what to do. The Clot was a very singular thing. In the end they agreed that she would leave her email address at the shop, and the assistant would consult others. Just before she left the assistant, with a sudden movement that surprised her, grabbed her hand over the counter and told her, whatever she did, she must stop the thing getting onto the bed again, because that bit was the weirdest and the most fucked up. They held hands for a while and she looked, quite enraptured, at the assistant's teeth, before nodding and leaving the shop.

She did feel guilty that evening as she stretched cling-film over the bowl. She watched as condensation appeared on the clear thin plastic, and coagulated into droplets. She took a fine point pen and poked some very tiny holes in the film, like you would do for an insect.

She woke up several times in the night, and ran her fingers blindly over the bedspread. But there was nothing there, and she retreated gladly back into her dreams, which that night were eccentric but not overly frightening. She dreamed, for instance, that she ate a huge bowl of pink spaghetti. She was woken up by the wire in her pelvis and her head and dragged herself into the bathroom. Nothing seemed to be happening to her body, except the pain. She opened her mouth wide, looking for something in her throat. She sat on the toilet bent over, squeaking slightly. Her phone was in her hand, and she hovered over her ex's number before pressing a button and turning the screen dark. She looked for painkillers in the cabinet, which had a faint smell left behind by the Clot, and found some of the stuff Hartley had been given for her bad back. She took two. Returning to her room, she realised that it was full of the same smell as the cabinet.

In the morning she went over to the bowl were the Clot lived and saw it had pushed through the small hole she had made; edging down the side of the small table it was resting on.

She peeled off the film and put the Clot on her sill to give it some air. Beneath the window the leaves of the vine were crowding in on something, as carnivorous fish might a corpse drifting down onto the ocean floor. Once again she thought of throwing it out into the garden, letting it fight things out with the vine, or be redly absorbed into the soil. But what if someone (Hartley) found it? Once again she reflected that it had not, necessarily, asked to be here. She worried it wanted to get back inside her. Perhaps she should let it. The doorbell rang.

Outside there was a man with a package, addressed to her. He wanted her to sign for it, which she did before taking it in both her hands (the package was large) and bringing it warily into the house. The package had her ex's handwriting on it.

The box was taped up, and she used a dinner knife to get it open. She found her things, jumpers, socks, clothes that she had left behind. There was some underwear that didn't belong to her. Then, a rustling of paper: gifts? Wrapping paper, carefully folded but not taped around a great number of the objects in the bottom of the box. She lifted one out – the paper was a pattern she thought she recognised. It was creased round a book, white marks where the tape had pulled the pattern away. She remembered picking it out in the shop, uncertain, when their love was new. She found a fresher bundle, this one she definitely recognised: her home made Christmas paper from last Christmas, marbled candy colours. In it, a bottle of expensive (she had saved to buy it) perfume, barely used. She took out each bundle, rewrapped in the paper she had wrapped it in. She laid out each gift she had given to her ex across the floor. Some items were broken, some containers empty. Everything that could come back had been returned.

The wires pulled taught and slack. She made herself a cup of herbal tea. Perhaps she let it stew for too long; the brew was incredibly bitter. She finished the tea anyway and, seconds later, vomited without warning or intent. She was taken so much by surprise that she didn't make it to the bathroom, instead spewing brackish water into an empty pint glass beside her bed. Next to the glass sat the Clot in its bowl, still looking profoundly organic, grotesquely alive. She extended one finger and placed it on the Clot. Something moist attached itself to her hand, trailing away as she pulled back. The pain increased in pitch: a long high note. She heard the key in the front door, Hartley, probably, back from work. What would Hartley make of the layout on the floor? She heard feet coming up the stairs, and grabbed the bowl with the Clot in it (water, stained with its mucous, splashed down her front and onto her feet), and held it close to her body. The smell that came out of it was stronger than ever, the smell seemed to crawl up into her nostrils and she clapped her hand over the bowl's wide mouth too late as the Clot slipped over the rim, hit the floor with a soft squelch, rolled under her bed and disappeared from sight.

Perhaps like the presents, the Clot was a thing returned. She thought of what she and her ex had done. Sacrifices, human and animal. The many, many arguments in McDonalds after midnight. She thought of the time they grew an avocado from a pit, suspending it in a jar of water– the jar becoming jumbled and busy with the avocado's white and brown roots. Was that the life the Clot had lived inside her?

Perhaps, she thought, the Clot had not emerged whole, and there was more to come, one way or another. They had lit a candle in a blue dish, and kept it burning for thirty days and nights. In pursuit of an outcome that she had now forgotten.

Sucker
———

On weekend mornings, she makes the coffee. This Sunday she's pissed off in a mixed way, meant to get up earlier and get more done, but she knows that's not Jay's fault. It just feels like it is. The feeling is hard to ignore, but so is this *happiness* which now intrudes. The anger is in her head, the happiness is in her body, in the way she's leaning against pillows, in the way she can feel a portion of him against her side. The bedroom curtains are orange, a coral kind of orange. They stain the room with cheerful, vitamin radiance.

There isn't - hardly ever - a day she doesn't look at these curtains and feel glad she chose them. The fabric really is just right. These curtains are almost perfect: the way they hold light in at night and invite it through themselves come morning.

As she watches this orange-stained winter light come in, lapping against their bedroom walls, a memory of the previous night wells up in her, climbing up her throat and roiling about on her tongue. The dream is bitter like metal, salty in the disturbing, toothsome way of blood. Something in her dream was coming up out of the darkness, gaining on her from below, fighting elegantly with itself. Something like a bolus of vegetation, trailing fronds or... But she cannot look at the dream straight on and, when she tries, it disappears. It is a phantom in this uncompromising, smiling, orange bedroom. It cannot compete with the broad, thermal-vested flank of the man beside her. That known flesh, still very warm and stale from sleep. Feeling a wave of compassion for him, she wants to bite, but mustn't, she turns and sucks, sucks on his skin with her mouth, a little sucker.

Lower, Jay says, stroking her hair.

She isn't young to have become a mother, not at all. Thirty years old is not young for that and Jay, even, is older. But still she feels that they are young, and poorly suited in many respects. With her mouth over his dick, she fights for breath like under a wave, like when she first went surfing in rough sea as a child. She learned to hold her breath and stay under when she came off, so the current wouldn't ram the board straight into her head. She learned to wait for the wave to pass over before coming up. Because the sea is rough and will kill you with a surfboard to the skull. She controls her breathing around his dick and thinks of how they fit each other better now than when they met. Certainly better than in those long days of attrition after the Little Bastard's birth, when she discovered that special genus of despair, despair smothered by love. Orange light washes over her body, through a gap between the duvet and the mattress. She shifts under the bedclothes, struggles slightly to gain purchase. After it's over he uses his hand for her, and she manages, briefly, to disappear.

They lie side by side for a few moments, then she gets up and tugs the curtains open, gently, just a little. She knows he hates it when she throws them suddenly apart. She peeks through the gap she has made: the sky is broad and bright. Oh, the day really *is* starting too late, but she does not say so. Something else they have discussed is that, yes, she needs to relax. So, she will relax. What plans do they even have today? No plans, except being together. There is still plenty, plenty, plenty of time for that today. He is talking, and she is not listening to him, but that is fine. That's OK. They are both looking at their phones, ignoring the small noises coming from floor below. He is awake, then, their Little Bastard, residing in a place of happiness and fear. They know they shouldn't call their son that, even between themselves, but it's too funny. You have to be so *nice* to your children, and quite often the Little Bastard, who is entertaining himself in the mysterious way he does on Saturday mornings, directing his toys into perverse dramas, doesn't deserve it.

She makes her way downstairs. The routine for today is well established. What if she were to refuse her part in it? But, oh, it is such a small part. Its smallness is, in fact, the point: *let Mum have a lie-in.* Although, really, she still gets up first to make the coffee. She prefers it that way, anyway, treading alone and carefully into the newest set of hours. But soon she will be back upstairs in bed and then, *then,* the special Father Cookery of weekends will begin.

She passes the closed door of the Little Bastard's room, hears him speaking his own language to an entourage of animals and trucks. She creeps the rest of the way to the kitchen and closes the door. The percolator lies, disassembled, on the draining board. Silver aged to a dull grey. With familiar movements she hefts the broad base, fills it with cold water and slots in the delicate cradle. Coffee, scooped into the cradle with precision, must form a cone of powder, loosely packed, not pressed. The head screws on with its jutting spout, the hinged lid pleated like a fan. She puts the percolator on the hob and turns the flame up beneath it. It is so cold in the kitchen this morning that her breath is visible. The floor is so cold her feet push themselves away from it by the arches, trying to curl up into themselves. She stands at the kitchen counter between the cooker and the sink and looks out of the window. She uses a finger to draw something in her own condensed spit on the pane in front of her, wriggling tentacle-like lines.

She is not looking, not really, at the row of shops and flats on the other side of the street. The smell of the coffee reminds her, oh, as it always reminds her, of a balcony, ten years ago or more now. She was sitting on that balcony alone, drinking coffee. Above her head a row of damp t-shirts were hanging on a line, square and white, like a string of flags. It was autumn, she was so young, she was wearing a square, white t-shirt. Through the mesh that covered the balcony, for the prevention of birds and suicides, she saw the tops of trees. Leaves, turning with the season into shades of saffron, lemon and apricot, lay against their dark wet branches. The owner of all the t-shirts was very close, just inside the door to the balcony, sleeping on a mattress on the floor. It was she, mattress sleeper, t-shirt owner, who taught her to make coffee, the way she makes it still.

The percolator is joggling excitedly on the hob and making a sputtering noise. It adds its own steam to her breath, which eclipses the drawing on the windowpane. The percolator, oh, such a *small* artefact when compared with the whole mess of the year of shirts and balconies. But it is one of very few things which survived the moves and upsets and subsequent loves, which has survived the coming of the Little Bastard. Behind the door on the other side of the hall, some toy of her son's goes *snicker snack*.

Jay smells the fresh coffee. He appears as she is carefully pouring it into mugs, opening the door so expansively that she cringes a little. He approaches her from behind, clasping her shoulders. Together they look through the window. He rubs his chin against her neck.

She takes her coffee up the stairs, leaving behind her the clanking of pots and pans, many more than this meal will require. Getting back into bed, she hears the sound of her partner and her son greeting each other: one voice high, one low. Her phone vibrates and, when she glances at the screen, something sharp and ugly stirs up in her gut. Instinctively she turns the phone face down. With some thankfulness she picks up the thing she has been saving to read, unfolds its luxurious, wing-like, pages and finds an article about octopuses. Octopi? The article begins with a description of a famous print, one which depicts a woman having sex with, not one, but *two* of these arresting creatures. The description is followed by a photograph of, according to the caption, a Giant Pacific octopus. It reclines upon the seabed; it has a great, wise, crimson head. Its tentacles are raised as if asking for a dance, or threatening violence. As she looks, she thinks she will dissolve. She reads about the habits of octopuses, their intelligence. She learns that their skin, which is not skin in the way that hers is, has pixels like a television, is capable of fabulous displays. She reads that octopuses can see with their skin, maybe think with it. That their blood is blue and green. She is slightly short of breath. Her face is hot: is she blushing?

When the high and low voices call for her, she drags herself back into the body which belongs to them. She folds the article carefully, back along its crease, storing it beneath the books and half-drunk cup and glasses on her bedside table.

Breakfast is a slightly charred omelette with mushrooms, bacon and green onion. The Little Bastard picks the bacon out with his fingers and eats that first, while Jay eats his portion in large, indiscriminately hot-sauced, bites. She talks to each of them in a similar tone about what they will do that day. In her brain, tucked behind a folded bank of synapses, she secretes a large, temperate ocean paved in yellow sand and rich in coral. The octopus, tentacle by roving tentacle, emerges from an orifice of rock. She feels something on her knee, Jay's hand. Egg begins to spackle the table and the floor around her son.

They bundle up and go on a walk. The path they take, the path they always take, runs alongside a canal. Their son likes to look at the boats and the birds. Some way along the brown water, they will reach a playground tucked into the side of a small, scrubby hill. If they went further the canal would meet a river, and the path would run alongside a wide expanse of marsh. She used to walk alone on that marsh, oh, almost daily. She toiled across it in her pregnancy, pissed in bushes, walled in by elderflower and spreading vines of morning glory. But she knows already that today they will not reach the marsh. The afternoon is disappearing inside this small playground, the spectacle of her son on the monkey bars, held up by his father, jumper riding up to reveal a bare, chubby little waist. As she watches them, her sight is suddenly clouded. She tastes the blood-like taste again, and the urge to escape, to spilt, to retreat in one great frothing rush, is almost irresistible. She gets a grip, waves to her child as he approaches her. She tugs his clothing into place, pushes his arms back into his coat. Whose arms does she push into the coat? They are her son's arms, his arms belong to her. The soft inside of his elbows: blue veined. He doesn't know he has got cold. She knows it for him.

That night she lies in bed while Jay pulls the curtains back together, ready for the onset of sleep. From this angle the pleats of orange fabric, dimmed to red, form long tubes like the muscles of a great throat. She's too tired, of course, to read, but before she closes her eyes, she reaches out and touches the paper folded on the table beside her. Jay tuns his light off and rolls over: she feels the heat of his body before it reaches her, engulfing, in the dark.

The next day, Monday, she picks her son up from nursery. The nursery's feral smell has transferred to him, just as it always does. For dinner she has decided, fuck it, on fish fingers, treat for them both. Her day has not been easy. She meant to wait for Jay and eat with him, but instead finds herself sitting down with the Little Bastard. They have matching plates, patterned with cats holding instruments. The benign fish oblongs are accompanied by potatoes, broccoli and ketchup. She entreats him to dispense the sauce with caution, and he tries. She puts a fish finger in her mouth and finishes it as her child muddles a bite around all his small white teeth. They are very fucking small, her child's teeth. The taste is pleasure everywhere, in her toes. But what if there is a bone in one of the pieces, and what if he swallows the bone? But of course, he has not swallowed a bone.

Later she falls asleep deeply and easily, staring at their

throat-like curtains, running a finger along the crease of her folded article. A few hours later she wakes up full of horror. Tears on her face, creeping into her mouth. She is so frightened; she can barely move. Slowly, slowly her fingers dare to cross the mattress, her whole body following them round and pressing up against Jay till she is holding the full real body of him. The dream (a familiar one: unknown persons torturing her child) recedes, her thoughts creep back to their usual positions. To ward off the darkness she pictures a time at the beach, a real memory of the sea, waves sharp and clear as cut gemstones. No sand, only the hot rocks, blaze of their happiness, warm bread and beer. The sun a sheet of metal on their bare backs. But that was before the Little Bastard. She feels disloyal and the dream has shaken up her superstitions. She conjures up another summer, after he was born, she sat him on her lap, his face barely clearing the table, and she fed him with her fingers, like putting food into her own mouth, the smell of his hair…

But she is still *so* frightened.

She has work tomorrow and now she's awake in the middle of the night, probably, for she won't even look at the time. Oh she will. Oh she could sleep for three more hours if she went to sleep right now, which she won't. She rolls away from Jay, who, in his undisturbed sleep, resembles nothing so much as heap of warm, dumb, earth. She reaches for her phone and, without really meaning to, begins watching videos with the sound off. Little square videos. Look! An octopus! Roiling on the white bottom of a boat it spreads its redness like a stain. It curls and it uncurls. Someone puts a hand on its head and leaves a pale hand-print. The hand-print makes her seethe with rage. She imagines touching an octopus on the mouth, at the meeting of its legs, and falls asleep with the phone in her hand.

When the alarm goes off she jerks, and the phone jumps across the bed. Jay will take their son to nursery that morning, it is his day off, his day in general to deal with the Little Bastard, who loves his dad so much. Wants to be carried, arms up in a beseeching loop, and Jay often does carry him. She has this instinct, sometimes, to tell him not to carry their child, not to spoil him, to keep his legs strong and his spirit independent, but she dismisses this instinct as basically wrong.

The bus, its incessant roaring and beeping, drives her into a defensive stupor. Her face against the glass, every pore feels a little bit of condensation drip in, smeary steam coming into her skin. Octopuses, she has read, seem sociable, yet are solitary. It baffles their observers. She thinks it is simple – they are enough for themselves. Their whole bodies are brains: too much, she thinks, loving someone else is too much for an octopus. On her phone, another square video, this time of small octopuses being cooked in a pan. They wriggle, curl up, turn deep purple. She remembers her nightmare. The Little Bastard. Arms outstretched for his dad to carry.

She ends up leaving work early. Someone had made her a cup of tea, she barely looked up as it was put by her elbow. But when she did sit away from the screen, leaning back with her hands around the rim, she noticed that one of her fingers had begun to droop, as if boneless. Had it melted against the hot cup? But it wriggled, ever so slightly, blood flushed into it for a moment turning it carmine red. The next moment a finger again. Only minutes later, eyes back on the screen, it occurred to her that something was not quite right.

Walking from the tube at dusk there are stripes of light on the walls of Costcutters. Oysters laid on iced troughs in front of the fishmongers. Their sparkling ice bed seems strangely optimistic. Through the door of the corner shop, she sees the print of newspapers, great black letters of headlines. Something terrible.

That evening she has a bath before leaving the house. That the evening will contain these two activities, bathing and leaving the house, astonishes her. She and Jay are going out, and they have a babysitter. The Little Bastard is totally in love with her, so much so he is afraid of his parents' departure. She feels the desperation in his small, pyjama-clad protest: *Mum can I come?* She remembers the helplessness of a wild, child's, love and sympathises: he is not sure what he will do, left at home with his passion. Will he strip naked? Throw up with excitement? But oh, she and Jay are heartless, and leave him with the babysitter.

A bit drunk in the lovely private darkness of the cinema, she thinks of the ex-girlfriend, invisible sleeper of her memory, who gifted her the percolator. One of several people she thought would be the last she'd love. Sitting there with

Jay's arm around her, she feels unbearably happy, unbearably sad. The film is not good. Should she reach for his dick, now, here? They wouldn't miss anything. Seems a risky move though, risky in the sense of will they be caught and risky, like, will he go for it?

The old girlfriend, who in fact is very young compared to her, how reduced she seemed in that hospital bed. Purple, the ends of her fingers, one squeezed by the end of a strange plastic clip, taking the measure of something inside her, its levels or frequency. The text which preceded yesterday's hospital visit: emoji skull, an emoji syringe half full of ominous green liquid, emoji skull.

In the cinema Jay takes her hand and presses it briefly against his face. He doesn't know about the ex who now lies in the hospital, although why she's kept it from him, she's not sure. An error of judgement early on, not necessary. What about her who he meets once or twice a year for drinks when she's in town? Her, who once stayed on their sofa for two nights, who held the Little Bastard as a baby and said: *Fuck! He's got your eyes darling!*

But silence gives birth to silence, a small but resilient population of lies. Too late now to tell him that grief and regret are on their way, will soon engulf her and so him, and then their son most likely. She wants to protect them. She can't though.

His ex-girlfriend's elegant fingers pressed against the soft cloth of the baby-gro, fingers lightly digging as she jogged the (Very) Little Bastard on her knee.

In the hospital her own old love said to her: *I never met your son!*

Almost certainly won't ever now. But these things happen. All these things have happened: the woman dying in that hospital bed taught her that when you make coffee in a percolator, make sure the dry grounds form a peak. The hand, its fingertips now purple and one clipped, that whole hand once was inside her, finger by finger. Jesus to think how careful she was, how gentle and teasing, when the Little Bastard just tore his way out in the other direction, skull like a wet red battering ram.

She feels her legs begin to lose their bones in the dark, and drool and wiggle into the gaps under the armrests. She thinks, ignoring the film, about how octopuses sometimes reach out and take the hands of divers. She, too, one day, in a hospital bed. She should check more often those parts which must be checked, she should practice more often the habit of safety, not take dark roads at night. Oh, what would happen to her son? Inevitably she falls asleep in the cinema.

Soon after laying eggs a female octopus starts to die. Holes appear in her, like tears in muslin. The male dies after mating too, usually they get eaten, drifting dejectedly and without purpose through the cruel ocean. Thinking of this she looks fondly at Jay as they leave the cinema, cross the road to the bus stop. Her phone vibrates in her back pocket. She still has white lines, across her belly and thighs from when her son grew inside her. Apparently, octopus fucking is when the male, very carefully, on the end of his arm, passes over a bag of sperm. He doesn't want to get bitten.

Octopus.

Octopus.

She has stopped in the middle of the road while she looks at the lit screen of her phone, flashing the octopus emoji, vibrating insistently. A light breeze along the pavement picks up into the crowns of the trees that line the street, which roar into an ocean-like frenzy. She stands between the lines of pitching trees as if in the valley of two crests of wave.

Octopus.

Octopus.

The vibration of the phone is waves within waves, the insistent current of a different sea. For a vertiginous moment, the one before you come off the board and it barrels into your head, the past lays itself out differently for her, she has done everything differently and she never made it here to this street, this cinema, this partner, this grief, and this child.

Octopus

Octopus

She stands in the middle of a road which is empty but will not remain so. A wave of sufficient velocity can have an impact on the human body equivalent to that of a speeding vehicle.

Octopus

Octopus

He is waiting for her on the other side of the street, calling to her from the pavement, calling her name.

Acknowledgements

Thank you so much to Aaron Kent and Broken Sleep Books.

Thanks to my friends and family, chosen and given.

LAY OUT YOUR UNREST

Milton Keynes UK
Ingram Content Group UK Ltd.
UKHW020612050923
428080UK00010B/249

For Maria

Fraternally

[signature]

Global History

A View from the South

Through the voices of the peoples of Africa and the global South, Pambazuka Press and Pambazuka News disseminate analysis and debate on the struggle for freedom and justice.

Pambazuka Press – www.pambazukapress.org

 A Pan-African publisher of progressive books and DVDs on Africa and the global South that aim to stimulate discussion, analysis and engagement. Our publications address issues of human rights, social justice, advocacy, the politics of aid, development and international finance, women's rights, emerging powers and activism. They are primarily written by well-known African academics and activists. All books are available as ebooks.

Pambazuka News – www.pambazuka.org

 The award-winning and influential electronic weekly newsletter providing a platform for progressive Pan-African perspectives on politics, development and global affairs. With more than 2,500 contributors across the continent and a readership of more than 660,000, Pambazuka News has become the indispensable source of authentic voices of Africa's social analysts and activists.

Pambazuka Press and Pambazuka News are published by Fahamu (www.fahamu.org)